For Isabel . . . in the middle

Henry Holt and Company, *Publishers since 1866*
Henry Holt® is a registered trademark of Macmillan Publishing Group, LLC
120 Broadway, 25th floor, New York, NY 10271
mackids.com

Library of Congress Cataloging-in-Publication Data
Names: Denise, Anika, author. | Denise, Christopher, illustrator.
Title: Bunny in the middle / Anika Denise ; illustrated by Christopher Denise.
Description: First edition. | New York : Henry Holt and Company, 2019. |
"Christy Ottaviano Books." | Summary: Illustrations and easy-to-read text
celebrate the joys of being the middle child in a loving family of rabbits.
Identifiers: LCCN 2018039226 | ISBN 978-1-250-12036-6 (hardcover)
Subjects: | CYAC: Middle-born children—Fiction. |
Brothers and sisters—Fiction. | Family life—Fiction. | Rabbits—Fiction.
Classification: LCC PZ7.D41495 Bun 2019 | DDC [E]—dc23
LC record available at https://lccn.loc.gov/2018039226

Our books may be purchased in bulk for promotional, educational, or business use.
Please contact your local bookseller or the Macmillan Corporate and Premium Sales Department at
(800) 221-7945 ext. 5442 or by email at MacmillanSpecialMarkets@macmillan.com.

First edition, 2019 / Book designed by Patrick Collins
The artwork for this book was created with paper and pencil; Adobe Photoshop; and Procreate
on iMac and iPad. The artist also used an Apple Pencil and a Wacom tablet.
Printed in China by Toppan Leefung Printing Ltd., Dongguan City, Guangdong Province

1 3 5 7 9 10 8 6 4 2

BUNNY
in the Middle

Anika A. Denise

illustrated by Christopher Denise

Christy Ottaviano Books

Henry Holt and Company ✦ New York

When you're in the middle...
you're not the oldest
and you're not the youngest.

You
are
right
in
between.

There's someone bigger
who helps you

and someone smaller who needs you.

When you're in the middle...

you know when to hold on,

when to let go . . .

and how to solve sticky situations.

When you're in the middle...

sometimes you lead,

sometimes you follow,

and sometimes . . .

you go your own way.

Being in the middle isn't always easy.
You get hand-me-down everything.

And you *never* get your own room.

But that's okay.
Because when you're in the middle . . .

you're not too small for the big stuff

and not too big for the small stuff.

But the best part of middle is . . .

you

are

loved

all

around.